LEGUMES

Gabriela Knutson

with illustrations by Diana Kohne Kenny

www.gabrielaknutson.com/legumes

ISBN 978-1-927967-59-1

To my handsome husband and
beautiful kiddos, Alice and Eddie.

And to my brother, who will live in my heart forever.

Table of Contents

Detection

"I concur."

That's all he tells me (sometimes he says "kinky is the way for me" but only during the most inopportune moments, so it doesn't count).

Would you prefer Indian or Thai? – "I concur."

Peanut butter or chocolate chip? – "I concur."

Your place or mine? – "I concur."

The detection of his volatile emotions is key to understanding this man completely, wholly and without a doubt. I use a portable radio with a large, obtrusive antenna to decrypt the true intentions of his stare and the meaning behind his agreeability. Every Sunday I print out a report which extrapolates, through complex mathematical equations, the intricate and often juxtaposed articulations of his brain.

At last, I can retrieve meaningful answers to my inquiries: Thai. Chocolate chip. His place.

He doesn't seem to mind me following him around with the apparatus as long as it doesn't accidentally pick up signals from the local radio station or disturb his aging cat, who, I've come to realize through long hours of research, doesn't really like the hard-wood floors or the color orange.

Although the truth only exists in the algorithms of the past and I am constantly made to wonder about the present, I am fascinated by the notion of a future guaranteed to be laminated with long hours of solving the calculus that is him. That, and the French radio station I pick up every once in a while.

Oh-la-la.

Marbles

Each day came by with a bang or two of sorts. The girl who always sat in the corner of the school yard where all the dead moths gathered for some reason, never seemed to mind the constant humming of the principal's ventilator near the window. She sat there all throughout recess listening to the children playing in the distance. She would close her eyes and listen to the colorful sounds of the chain on the swing and the thump-thump of the children's sneakers on the metal slide.

Little sounds she liked. The whispers between little girls and their quiet giggles afterwards, the screams of little boys catapulting themselves off the monkey bars and their landings on the sand, or the courageous kid flying away from the swing in full thrust, in full swing.

All those sounds kept the balance of the world. That's why Mr. Coupe's ventilator never bothered her.

Neither did the thought of the whispering and giggling being about her, which was the case most of the time. Sometimes, it was about Gustav and his missing eye. Gustav had a tendency to lose his glass eye. His real eye was lost when he was three in a Karaoke incident which he doesn't recall. Often the nuns had to help him look for his blue glass eye in the sand but Ritchie and his friends would find it first and play with it after school. The nuns usually gave up and escorted Gustav to the nurse's office where he would wait for a replacement.

Over the years, Ritchie and his friends collected a large number of Gustav's eyes. They carried them around in their pockets and used them as marbles in the playground. The clicking sound of the glass eyes in Ritchie's pocket in particular fascinated the girl, who called herself Carrie even though her real name was Sandy Deen.

In her corner of the playground, she waited patiently for Gustav to lose another eye and for Ritchie to collect it. She couldn't wait to hear the wonderful and exquisite melodies that would be born into existence when yet another white and blue sphere would join the countless others in Ritchie's pocket. In secret, she loved Gustav and Ritchie equally and deeply for giving her this unique and everlasting memory.

Over the years, Carrie tried in vain to replicate that glorious sound. She even went so far as to bribe a doctor into selling her a pair of glass eyes, but it just wasn't the same. To this day, Carrie still closes her eyes and remembers the exceptional, unexplainable sound of glass colliding against glass, like a small, colorful creature living inside Ritchie's pocket.

Every so often, she walks by the ol' playground and digs in the sand gently with her fingers just to see, just to see.

To Perendinate

One day, for no decipherable reason, Julie decided to hold all calls, all interviews and appointments. She even gave her assistant the rest of the day off. She wanted to just sit calmly behind her desk, on her comfortable green chair with the worn fabric on the armrests and stare.

Two big deadlines were, for now, forgotten and put aside. The suffocating pressure of urgent deliverables slowly fizzled out of the window she opened. Her view of a small but green manicured yard was perfectly framed by a fig tree. She reached out and plucked one right off the branch, scattering leaves all around.

Sweet, purple and delicious, the fig disintegrated in her mouth. How long had it been since she had a fig? It had been years. This whole time they had been growing right outside her window within reach.

The sound of the phone ringing broke her contemplative stare and she slowly reached for the receiver and dropped it. She could almost hear the faint "Hello? Hello?" coming from the dangling artifact on the other side of her desk.

It crossed her mind that this could just be an excuse to perendinate and not complete the idiotic marketing campaign that was assigned to her for a couple of days. Her instincts told her otherwise. The moment she dismissed Elsie and set her out-of-office, she felt a surge of liberation and a tingle of excitement.

In five years, she had not missed a deadline, an email, a phone call, or an appointment.

"Why now?" she pondered as she tried to get a piece of fig skin out from between her teeth with her fingernail.

This reminded her why she hated figs and why she had sworn she would never eat another one again. She sighed, closed the window and reached for her phone.

"Elsie, I changed my mind. Bring me a double espresso and some floss, pronto." She hung up.

Those were the happiest four minutes of her life.

Bowling Night

"Take me bowling," I said to him, trying to make him laugh. "I want to sit in the pretty chairs and enjoy a cold one while I watch you score some fantastic gutter balls. I want to watch you lose to me. Again."

He laughed a sad but hearty laugh as he drove his 50's Ford pick-up with the bad seat belts. He put his beer between his legs and his arm around me. I could smell the cheap cologne on his neck and felt his prickly beard against my cheek. I laughed and pulled away.

He had just dropped off his daughter halfway between El Paso and Ft. Worth. The little girl hadn't said a word the whole time. She held on to her raggedy doll as she stared outside, at the vacant desert all around us. She knew her time with daddy was up.

He had been careful driving with her in the car to the gas station where her mother waited. On the way back, however, all safety precautions were forgotten. We sped back, passing cars at a 90 miles per hour, not turning on the headlights when the last of the sunlight dissipated in the horizon.

I was 14 years-old the first time I saw him. He walked into my friend's house and made his way towards me with the porch light shining brightly behind him. Like an apparition, he was glowing. And like an apparition he remained throughout my life – surprise visits and quick goodbyes, but never even so much as a kiss.

That night, as we made our way back to the city on the deserted highway, I looked over at him – his face pale but full of anger and despair. I wanted so much to touch him, his thick black hair, his lips, but I knew that if I moved even an inch closer to him, there would be no turning back.

Before I could make up my mind, he took the next exit, drove down a dirt road, and stopped the truck before a locked gate. He threw the door open and ran in front of the headlights. With his fists up in the air, he screamed into the pitch black night with so much pain and desperation. He yelled, then cried and then yelled some more. Once he was done, he stopped and looked up at the starry sky for a long time.

Back on the road, he was silent, as was I. He put on a Billy Joel song and said it reminded him of me and that he would play it every time he wanted to remember something beautiful. Again, he put his arm around me, and this time I didn't pull away. We drove back the rest of the way just like that, knowing that we would never hold each other like that again.

He did take me bowling that night, and after three strikes in a row, beat me by 74 points. I watched myself lose to him. Again.

Young and Toppled

Young and toppled, Marcia introduced herself to the janitorial services manager not long after her incriminating surgery had taken place. The man, lacking stature and girth, looked at her closely while slowly tapping his shoe. He felt the gum under his sole adhere to the floor and snap back, adhere and snap. He pictured it in his mind, the pink blob unwilling to let go of the rubber sole. Adhere and snap. He had inspected it this morning at his desk, and after considering the joy of its existence, he decided to keep it there, safe, under his shoe for the rest of the day.

As Marcia continued to explain her background, including an all-inclusive fictional account of her horrible accident in the subway earlier that week, the manager began to ponder if the gum was still flavorful. Was it sugar free gum? Was it inside one of those massive gum machines once, waiting idly by, until its turn came to roll down the plastic spiral and pop onto the hand of an ungrateful brat only to be moistened for a second, then discarded like a dirty sock on the street?

The thought made him gag a little and sigh.

Marcia's little voice unnerved him so he stopped her mid-sentence and told her enthusiastically to sit down and listen. He only had one question, one question alone, one which would decipher who the perfect person for the cleansing operative position would be.

Marcia listened closely. She leaned forward a little and folded one of the bandages up, revealing her small, pink ear, in order to absorb the question entirely. A question which would determine her fate.

He waited a second for her to adjust before he cleared his mind, throat and pants, which were covered in food particles from his lunch just 10 minutes before.

"What would you like me to ask you?"

After a brief pause, the manager told her to think about it.

"What do you really want me to know about you?"

Contemplating on the nature of the question and deciding that it was indeed a trick question, Marcia opted to fold the bandage back to cover her ear and fold up the one covering her left eye, so that she may see his expression more clearly.

As her eye adjusted to the light, the manager came into focus after a short while. He sat there, dwarfed by the size of his chair. She noticed a large white poster board stapled crookedly on the wall behind him. In big, sloppy blue marker the words "MARLOW'S INN" were sprawled out indecently.

All she could do to stop herself from crying was to try to imagine what "Marlow's Inn" could be. She pictured a dark, smelly diner in downtown L.A. where all the patrons are vagrants and tired bus travelers from up north. Marlow's Inn. She could see herself almost ordering a small bowl of chili and a hot, black, thick cup of coffee with a crispy donut on the side.

Then, she looked at him again.

"I would like you to ask me about my calibration expertise and my ability to synchronize watches."

The words escaped from her without her will. She felt the b's, the s's, and all the vowels pass from her throat to her mouth to the room where the sound reverberated all around her.

There was an immediate spark of embarrassment and complete regret inside her chest accelerating the beating of her heart. Never had she bothered to look at her watch even once in all her life and calibration gave her a headache. There they were;

the two skills she never mastered were now gallivanting about the room with such pride and sin.

The janitorial services manager sank deeper into the brown aged leather of the chair. Marcia waited for a response. She couldn't help but think that it looked as though the chair was slowly digesting a tiny meal. Was it? It was!

The man just stared at her silently as he sank deeper and deeper until only his legs were visible.

Marcia struggled to get up from her chair and limped to his desk. That's when she noticed the gum stuck on his shoe. A piece of light pink, disgusting bubblegum stretching from the floor to his shoe was the only thing keeping the chair from swallowing him whole. Before she could reach him with her bandaged arm, the bubble gum snapped. In he went.

She stared in disbelief at the leather mass digesting the man who could have given her a job and hence a second chance. All she had now was a bad nose job, some cheek implants and a new mole. Tears flowed from her eyes and moistened the yellowing bandages, making them sag a little, revealing raw pink flesh here and there.

The whole gruesome affair seemed quite regal and dignified until the chair began shaking, then convulsing, contorting explosively all around the room until it expectorated the piece of gum, shooting it across the room from deep inside itself. Marcia and her wild reflexes reached and caught it with her good arm in mid air. The blob deflated and reconstructed itself under the Marlow's Inn sign, becoming a chair again; comforting, welcoming.

Marcia looked down at her closed fist and slowly opened it. The gum, pale pink and dry, looked insignificant in the scope of things. It also looked like the man who beat her. It was as though she held his little head in her hand. How soft, how malleable.

She dropped it on the floor, like he did her self-esteem, her courage, her conviction and stepped on it, delighting in twisting her foot all over it. The scars would eventually fade, but there, on her sole, the gum remained as a reminder of her escape, always and forever. Adhere and snap. Adhere and snap.

Tire Iron

Aunt Molly disemboweled her nephew's car and beat it senseless with its own tire iron. The Mustang never had a chance against the wrath of his lunatic aunt and her feverish anger. Sunny watched from inside his mother's house as his red dream bled oil and gas onto the pavement below. He stood motionless by the window for the hour and 17 minutes it took Aunt Molly to mutilate and destroy the car for which he had been saving most of his life.

In the end, she kicked the fender loose with her bare foot. Breathing heavily, she held the tire iron by her side and admired her work as the sun set behind her sister's house.

"There. No more nightmares. No more isolation," she whispered as she walked back.

The creaking of the door startled Sunny some, but he didn't take his eyes off the wreck outside. Aunt Molly walked toward him and ran her fingers through his dirty blonde hair. She held his chin with the tips of her fingers and kissed him on the cheek.

"Virtue is here to be seen, not heard," she said as she gently tapped him on the shoulder. She walked away, not really expecting a response.

He didn't look at her. He didn't move. The light of the sun faded away, leaving him in the dark and in silence until the sound of crickets outside filled the house slowly.

He held his driver's permit in his hand, perfect in every way. They even got his name right this time. I didn't even get to drive it, he thought.

"Dinner is ready! It's turkey, your favorite," his mother yelled from the kitchen.

Her voice awakened him from his stupor. He touched his pocket and felt the twenty dollar bill his father had given him the day before. He grabbed his cap from the couch and walked out of the house.

Off he went into the night and never looked back.

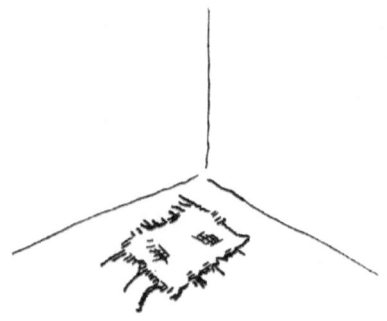

Marisol

Marisol grew each day more accustomed to the sound of the tic-tock clock in the living room. At first it infuriated her to be stripped away from the silence, but then, like the humming of the air conditioning unit, the sound melted into her subconscious and became nothing and everything.

There wasn't anything else to do in that house but sit in the cool living room with her doll and a sealed envelope on her lap. She stared out the window, towards the swaying tall trees in the distance behind Rita's house.

Of all the days, Mondays were the hardest to stay still, Wednesdays were okay and Fridays were the easiest. Her dress was always the same: flowery and soft with lace all over the place like a spider web tangled in a strong breeze.

For three years to the day, she remained sitting on the velvet couch with the silence in her head, amidst the rhythmic sounds which had become inaudible with time.

Her mother often sat beside Marisol and held her hand waiting for her daughter to say a word, any word, or maybe shift her gaze and look into her eyes. One day, without warning, Marisol walked into her mother's bedroom and requested a glass of milk, a glass of cold milk to accompany her cookies. Her mother picked her up in her arms, held her tight, and cried tears of happiness. "Of course, my darling! Anything you want."

Soon after, Marisol was enrolled in school and thrived in the classroom. She even made friends here and there, but every once in a while she would sit on that couch again and frighten her mother. One day, while Marisol was staying with Rita across the street, her mother destroyed the velvet antique with a hammer and a butter knife, threw the pieces in the car, and took it to the dump.

When Marisol returned from Rita's the following morning, all that remained was a small piece of red velvet fabric tucked away in the corner of the room. She picked it up before her mother came in and hid it in her pocket.

No one ever understood her fascination with silence and the overwhelming drive to be alone, if only for a couple of minutes a day. She tried to explain it to a few people – one friend, two boyfriends, her husband – but it was impossible for her to describe the complete feeling of ecstasy she felt while sitting completely still, alone, in silence.

Once, Thomas Gutierrez, a boy she dated briefly in high school, made her world spin around when he kissed her silently behind the lemonade stand she had built. He was mute. She was his. She thought he of all people would understand. But just as she was beginning to explain, the chilling noise gushing from the approaching ice cream truck ruined it all and she ran into her house crying, covering her ears with her hands. Thomas Gutierrez didn't call again.

When she was eighteen, Marisol lived by the ocean. She discovered the perfect place for her solitude: a forest that came dangerously close to the edge of the water. There she would sit, on a rock under a tree, and close her eyes and listen to the massive sound of the waves crashing below her, mist enveloping her and tickling her face. There she would feel what she felt on the velvet couch for three years of her life. That magical place is where she realized that silence was inside her and had made a permanent home in her body, had planted roots, deep into her soul and no matter where she went or how many people were around, she could always be alone.

This made her happy.

Desert Run

Lola told me to cool it or she would take me to the desert and beat me with all the popsicle sticks she had collected in her sleep. I wasn't paying attention to her, partly because she was French and partly because I was listening to a homeless man having a discussion with his penis as he urinated into a hole in the wall. I wanted to ask him to elaborate on his theory of evolution, but I couldn't find the right moment to interrupt the flow of the conversation.

The smelly little man insisted to hinder my sensibilities with his banter about Hell and the Resurrection – the two things I learned to avoid in my youth. I realized that the concept of coming back to life interested me a little more now that I was older, and when I turned to share my wonderful discovery with Lola, she was already yelling and spitting at the crowd of people who had assembled around her. As she was dragged away by the police, she shouted the alphabet in reverse, sprinkled with a few obscenities here and there, and skipped the letter P for some reason.

Hours later, her boyfriend Tommy bailed her out of the county jail and she walked home alone in the rain. She called me the next day to apologize. She said the mushrooms she had eaten had apparently been laced with PCP and she was suddenly horrified of limes.

I think she had been starved briefly in a former life, but that's just because Madame Turquoise told us so in one of her sessions. Madame also pinpointed the time of our deaths and I can't help but think how much Lola will miss me during those seven years we are apart.

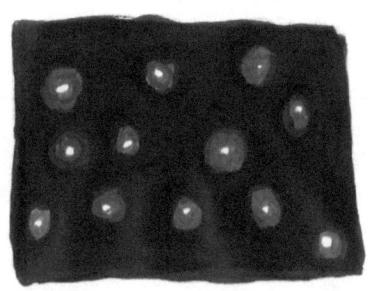

In El Paso

I remember that night clearly. I wasn't wearing my glasses and had been gutted and left for dead behind the Motel 8 on Stanton St. I remember staring at the underside of the garbage bin, liquid splashing joyfully onto the cement and thinking about how I was going to explain to the librarian why I hadn't returned "Crime and Punishment" by the due date and if she could possibly waive the fees this time.

I didn't want to look down at myself, at the pool of blood forming around me, so I inspected the crack on the bin with my fingers. Not so big, I thought. What could have caused it? Time, perhaps? Corrosive liquid dumped illegally? Was it just poorly manufactured?

The remote sound of sirens brought my attention back to the Motel 8 on Stanton St. Carefully, I touched where my belly should be and found a foreign sensation of numbness. There was no pain. I explored what I imagined to be my stomach…and this…this thing might be my lower intestine. How curious. It felt warm, wet, and soft, like seaweed floating by me while swimming in the ocean one summer in Costa Rica.

The sirens got closer and a voice behind me said "it's all right, lady. It's all right. The ambulance is coming." I just waved the voice away and I was once again floating in the pacific. I heard people yell and scream for me to get back to shore, but I ignored them all.

Float, float away, under the sun.

A flashlight blinded me and pulled me back to El Paso, the alley, the smell. I realized the liquid flowing from the container was yellow. I noticed the air was crisp and the stars were many as they picked me up and rolled me away to be stitched up in some hospital. Was it Providence? I think it was.

Alice and James and the Icebox

Alice is a girl who likes to jump rope in the morning before her breakfast jelly beans. She forgets who she is every evening and encourages her teddy bear to indulge in candy and coconut cream pie. To this day, Alice is terribly disgusted by cheese, particularly cheddar. It might be because she comes from a family of dairy farmers from Geltin, Pennsylvania, but who knows for sure.

Alice has a tendency to daydream about the boys she likes finding themselves in precarious circumstances. That's why she was under the impression that James had been buried in the ice box when in fact he was not. Just the other day, she imagined him chained to the gate in her backyard as Fluffy, her terrier, nibbled at the rotting sock on his lifeless foot.

Oh Alice. She's so tender in her daydreams.

James is a boy who lives across the street and torments her with his foul language and sour posture. His hair is reddish and curly and he gets goose bumps every time he sees a blue Cadillac speed by his house.

When James was in the third grade, he refused to write the letter "Q" in his writing exercises. He also didn't like to multiply any number by five. He said it made him feel queasy.

Often his mother was called to sit in the principal's office. Each time the principal would state that not only was James unruly, he had a distinct and citrusy odor about him.

From the office window, James would watch as his mother pulled into the school parking lot with her blue Cadillac and he knew that when she drove him home that afternoon, she would buy him an ice cream sundae with crushed almonds and a springy cherry on top.

Many years later, after Alice became a nurse for the elderly geese of her town and James declared himself sole proprietor of a snail circus, Alice decided to confess her perturbed, but honest love for him. James, in turn, asked her to marry him.

It was a simple ceremony in the town square, remembered for many years as the wedding with the miniature schnauzer band that lasted till noon the next day after a torrential storm.

They were married for many years and had two daughters and a son named Roy. This confused the children. They never knew who mom was referring to when she asked them to take out the trash, so they became known as Roy One, Roy Two, and Tom.

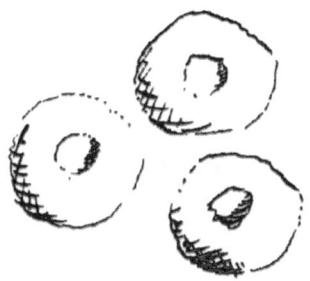

Cold Sarah

In winter she reminded me of my mother with those suffocating turtlenecks she loved so much. Maybe they reminded her of her life, making her inner pain and metaphorical strangulation physical. Or maybe she was just cold. Who can say?

At the park, she would hold my hand and laugh. Then she would start skipping, forcing my arm to swing back and forth because she knew it would make me angry. When I would let go and continue walking, she would stop in place and sulk.

"You know I don't like it when you do that," I would say to get her back to move.

Staring at the ground she would mutter "you're no fun," and then she would slowly lift her gaze and look at me straight in the eyes and very gently and softly whisper: "Beast." When she said that I felt like crumbling, like turning inside out and transporting myself somewhere else, far away, maybe at home on the couch, watching football, with her at my side holding a bowl of dry fruity Cheerios on her lap. That's where I would go in my mind, to those special moments when I was tolerable and she didn't think I was an ugly, hairy, insensitive beast.

I haven't seen her in ages. I can still remember the smell of her blond wispy hair resting on my shoulder and tickling my ears before I swapped it away, annoyed.

Sometimes, in the shower, I start singing "My Funny Valentine" out of tune and with the wrong lyrics like she used to do. The things I imagined doing to stop her racket every morning were many. I even bought a turtleneck recently – the same kind she gave me for my birthday and the same one I exchanged the next day for 2 pairs of socks and a watch.

I don't know if I'll ever wear it. I am slightly claustrophobic.

Swirl Envy

Sally enjoys living in Idaho, she says. She says the pomegranate trees in Ted's back yard are green with envy and treacherous in winter. The mailman told her once to keep quiet about the nightingale incident on Corner Ave. and Lincoln.

She never served tea at seven o'clock or ate biscuits after lunch. She kept her calendar clear of insects and walks to the zoo. She was terribly afraid of the letter "Z."

She waited idly by as the ice cream truck paraded down her formidable, yet statuesque block. How can the ice cream cone revolving atop the yellow polka-dot truck resent her so? The stern posture of the swiggle at the top unnerved her greatly.

Ted reassured Sally by twisting her hair around his finger and rhythmically patting her back.

She liked that. It gave her the willies.

The Kiss

Sometimes I listen to the refrigerator motor in search of her voice. I try to find her words in the low, rhythmic sound of the ailing machinery preventing the food inside from decaying too quickly. I press my cheek against the smooth, white surface, the vibration traveling all over my body, and I imagine what it would have felt like to have her hand caress my face softly. She did so only once, on the day she left my sister and I on my grandmother's porch, as the engine kept running on her El Camino.

The single letter she mailed, in which she explained in great detail how to bake an apple pie, contained the reason behind her disappearance: a guy named Tom. There was no apology, no regret, just a simple statement tucked away between sifting the flour and sweetening the apple filling. I read the letter over and over again until I memorized it, until her handwritten words, commas, and exclamation points had formed a sort of pattern that resembled my fading memory of her face.

All I knew about my mother came from that letter and muffled whispers I sometimes heard behind closed doors. From these few clues, I managed to construct a rough outline of her life, but that was not enough.

Everyday after school, I would rush to the kitchen and squeeze into the space between the refrigerator and the wall, where I created and imagined thousands of scenarios, an alternate reality where a relationship between us existed. Invented memories of my mother became the missing puzzle pieces needed to complete the landscape of my mother's life and to fill the void her absence caused in me.

Whimsy

Her name was Whimsy, she said, but Rita probably misheard her that night. Rita was a little drunk and a little pissy. Something happened to her rabbit's foot; probably lost it in the fire, but she wasn't sure.

That rabbit's foot was something special. Rita took that foot straight from her pet bunny Hilda while it was still alive many years ago. The voices told her to do it. They told her it was what Hilda really wanted, what she was born to do.

It wasn't as horrific as it sounds. The bunny had been given a large amount of alcohol three nights in a row to sedate her for the operation. During the procedure, Rita was very careful. She took the sharpest knife, sterilized it thoroughly with momma's gin, and waited until the bunny fell asleep on the cutting board. After taking a few more swigs of the gin to calm her nerves, Rita held on to the little foot and proceeded to slice it little by little so she wouldn't lose it like she did last time with her other bunny, Rupert. She used a hatchet that time and the foot went flying somewhere behind the stove.

When momma arrived home from work at the dairy farm, Rita was all done sewing Hilda up with the sewing machine, using her favorite crosshatch stitch. Momma didn't notice the blood, but the faint sounds coming from the bunny caught her attention slightly.

"What's wrong with Hilda, honey, or is that Rupert?" she asked, not really looking in her direction.

"Oh, Hilda's just coming out of anesthesia. She's a little cloudy."

"Ok. Good night, honey," she said and walked away with her gin.

Oh yes, that rabbit's foot certainly was special and now she was sure she left it on the coffee table next to her Good Housekeeping magazine and the pumpernickel muffin she was saving for later. If only she hadn't started that fire, she thought. If only the gas station attendant had been more helpful with the directions to the train station and charged her less for her cigarettes, then she wouldn't be in the back of her boyfriend's pick-up truck talking to Whimsy on their way to Mexico. Damn.

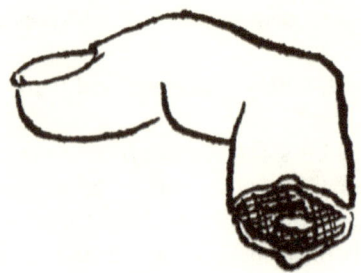

Lack

Linda doesn't lack anything these days, only her sense of humor and her pinky. She lost her pinky in a fight the other night when we were at the bar. She realized the girl behind her gave her a pinch and without thinking or remorse, slapped her a good one across the face. The girl, blonde and full of giggles, had great reflexes and quickly bit Linda's finger as it left her cheek and spit the tip of her pinky on her face.

"That's youth for you. Now have some soup," the girl said as she walked away from the counter. The girl, whose name was Eloise, ended up on the lap of some bohemian poet that night and had the best episode of the giggles yet. He wrote poetry in French on her inner thigh with a red fine point sharpie and misspelled the word "chanteuse" over and over.

The poet, ashamed of his infidelity to the English language, killed himself three years later by lacerating the area behind his knee with a dull knife he had used to spread mayonnaise on his crackers earlier that day.

When the neighbors found him in his apartment, they recalled hearing him say his last words with such sullen courage as he released his last breath.

"Oh death, I see thee now. Take my rice and spread it in Mongolia where there are no buffalo..."

Mr. McMahan, the building manager, later told his wife he hadn't heard anything at all, but because everyone else was gasping and awing, he gasped and awed too.

Quarrel Man

The individual in question had no idea where to begin his quarreling that afternoon. All objections seemed banal and all rhetoric inept. Everything else seemed blasé including the insult he endured in broken English when he refused to operate certain machinery in a convenience store around the corner.

On her doorstep he stood, defeated. Nothing to catapult his rage. Then, like a small miracle in July, he remembered the miniscule wrinkle on his tie he had to endure the entire day to the amusement of his office companions.

He remained poised on the porch, recalling every moment of embarrassment and shame to the last detail, feeding his anger and disgust until it ballooned to the perfect size and fervor. When he reached the climax of his rage, he opened the door and threw his briefcase across the hall, taking the flower vase with it to the floor.

"Is your only aim in life to destroy me, you wretched broom of a woman?" His roar vibrated throughout the house.

After a minute of silence, he heard the fluttering of small footsteps somewhere inside the kitchen cabinet.

He smiled and winked at himself in the mirror by the door. It turned out to be a good day after all, he thought.

He skipped merrily down the hallway, stepping on the broken vase and kicking his briefcase joyfully. He opened the closet door and stared vividly at a full set of tools, hooks and contraptions. After careful consideration and precise fondling, he chose, to the delight of the cat purring behind him on the couch, a tightly-coiled heavy wire, with discreet thorn-like spikes protruding at every angle.

It was a time of joy.

"Do you know what you did today, Ms. Prude? Do you know what suffering, shame and disruption you brought into my life with your imperfections?"

As he glided down the hall towards the kitchen, he pulled the coil apart with his bare hands. Here and there small beads of blood were born and smudged, and he, without flinching, proceeded to the kitchen cabinet.

He opened a small, wooden door underneath the stairs. He peered inside then reached into the darkness with his injured hand, feeling for her hair, like a spider web, thin and frail and dead.

Instead of feeling her struggle when he grabbed her tiny little useless head, her thin wispy hand grabbed his wrist gently. She pulled herself out of the little cabinet using his arm as support.

At first adjusting her eyes to the bright light, she brushed off the dust which had collected savagely onto her petite checkered dress and kissed the man on the cheek.

"I made meatloaf and mashed potatoes for dinner. You can nuke it later. I am going to the movies with Clare."

She walked past him, picked up her purse and left the house.

There he stood again, defeated.

One day, he thought. One day.

Up for Air

In the lake where I swam every day after school, I found treasures between the pebbles and the plant life. Treasures I would keep under my bed, next to the old transistor radio my father gave me for Christmas. My mom didn't approve of my random collection of trinkets and gold coins. Maybe she was jealous that I loved them more than I loved her; that I chose to be in my room all day organizing and cleaning the bounty instead of brushing her hair or talking about girlie things.

One year, when I went to summer camp she found the flimsy wooden box and gave it to the neighbor's kid Pete. That poor kid had to be taken to the hospital after he swallowed every single sparkly item. Pete had a weird walk after that and the neighbor didn't talk to my mother again. To punish me, she decided to sell the house and move to the city where the rats ate my food and the cockroaches took over my dresser.

Watching as the sun sets behind the high-rises, I want so much to dive into the chilly water once again, and search through the algae for more coins. I want to feel the water envelop me like my father did so long ago. At least, I imagine he did. I imagine he was a treasure hunter, an explorer who set out to discover other lands, leaving behind those hidden coins for me to find as proof of his existence, a promise of his return.

Highlight

Charlie was the highlight of the tour of the Alamo last summer. He had a set of green eyes of such lush candor, all I could do to keep from fainting was to repeat four Hail Marys, 15 national anthems (from 10 different countries) and to suck my cherry lollipop to the creamy center.

Charlie liked me, too, I could tell. He had nonchalantly pushed me behind a hay stack in the Alamo historical farm and taken a look at my intimates. Luckily, I wore my sister's good clean underwear that day. He told me how very surprised he was at the durability and stretchiness of the pink elastic waistband, as was I.

The Alamo holds a very important part in my heart to say the least.

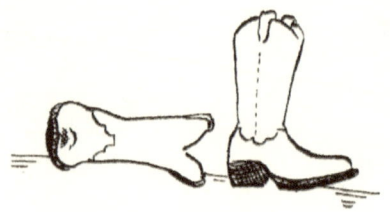

Boots

Sometimes Eddie called me into his room and reprimanded me for eating his grapes the night before. He would look at me with his droopy eyes and indulge me in the history of grape theft – from early Egyptian times to the wonderful world of today. I listened and rocked back and forth with my hands behind my back but all I could think about were the grapes I would surely steal the following week when momma went shopping for groceries.

Once he was done explaining why Sugar Ray became a boxer, he would tell me to help him get his boot off – the left one. He always had a hard time, so I did, help him, I mean. I would pull and tug and he would groan and kick until the darn thing came off. He would take his ostrich leather boot and look inside. Then he would take one long, strong whiff, and together we would say "Goodbye, gracious!"

Oh Eddie. I always remember him, just like that – passed out on his bed, clasping his boot tightly to his chest and then the long, disturbing wheezy snore that would be sure to follow.

Appetite

There is this little noise in her head that twinkles and sparks like a voltmeter on acid and slowly heightens in volume. It becomes deafening, the way reverberating thoughts can get.

"What's that? What did you say?" she would ask. "Oh sorry. It's the voices in my head. You are going to have to speak louder, louder than you've ever spoken before. Louder even. It is although you are mumbling something inside the barrel of a gun as I pull the trigger."

Tommy just gave up. He gave up trying to tell her sweet nothings and innocent whispers. Tommy gave up telling her she was beautiful only to lose to the voices in her head. So there he remained, silent on the couch. He imagined what it would be like if the world was silent, if no one was there to retrieve and analyze the encrypted sound waves. If only he spoke louder than they.

She made him happy with her smile and her darting blue eyes. But white and blue were not enough for Tommy. Like frozen dinners, it was not enough to fill the gaping appetite building inside him.

Patsy and the Postman

Patsy reminded me the other day about the time a watermelon was left on her doorstep. One morning, Patsy left her house to go to her employment agency job and tripped on the large, supple, juicy fruit. The fall caused her to break her wrist in three different places and dislocate her pinky. The neighbor, who everyone referred to as Sal, pointed in glee and hid behind his curtains.

She had assumed it was him. It wasn't.

The postman was the culprit. He had a sick sense of humor, that man. At night he would wait until his wife Helen was fast asleep and then he would put his face really close to hers. He stayed there, motionless, trying to contain his laughter, until she felt a presence, opened her eyes and found the eyes of a monster looking at her. Once she screamed so loud and punched him so hard in the stomach, he didn't speak to her for a week.

His wife never got used to the midnight pranks. One day she pretended to leave him to teach him a lesson. She packed all her clothes, her shoes and the lavender towel she loved and left the house. Heart-broken, the postman cried himself to sleep that night. She waited by the window of the bedroom until she was sure she heard him snoring. Helen then put on a Frankenstein mask she had purchased earlier that day at the liquor store and walked in slowly. Tip-toe, tip-toe.

She put her face really close to his. The hair on the mask tickled his nose and he opened his eyes.

The postman died of scurvy that night.

When Patsy heard the news of her postman's death, she knew it had been he who had candidly placed the watermelon on the porch. Her heart sank. She lived the rest of her days feeling guilty, with a strange aversion to English literature.

You don't say.

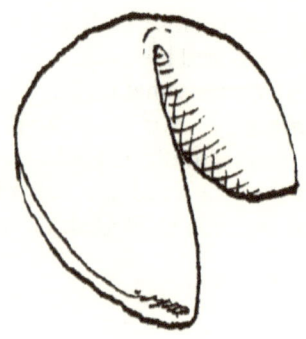

Bemoan

To bemoan is to be in a perpetual state of anxiety and to defeat the return of the hiccups. It also helps the insomniacs rinse the dishes while the rest of the world enjoys the brain as it archives the day's activities. All this I know because I read it once by chance in the boy's restroom while Tina lost her virginity for the third time and a half – I know, I counted, and nothing could dissuade me otherwise – unless it involves ice cream and gummy worms.

The knowledge one gains from the hieroglyphics rudimentarily splashed on to the smooth, shiny door of a bathroom stall is nothing but straight out fact – truth that has been tested, researched, and proven time and time again.

FOR A GOOD TIME CALL LINDSEY – that, my friend, is as good and as true as the day is long and my belly button is pierced.

Now, the fortune cookie – that's all BS. Don't believe that stuff no matter how much you feel that indeed "you should look inside for riches." I looked and all I found was goo. Goo is not riches.

Ludicrous

Ludicrous was what she said after the accident she witnessed the other day. The pig had been killed right in front of her. She was riding her bike at the request of Sister Helen. If she had walked like she always did, she wouldn't have been anywhere near the corner of 3rd and 5th. So there she was, riding her bike across the street when a man she didn't know stopped his truck at the light, tipped his hat, and said "miss" with a smile. She smiled back and watched as the man continued walking to the back of the truck. With grunts and tremendous force, he pulled a fascinating 500-pound pig down from the truck onto the street and shot him right there with a rifle.

The shooting had happened so close to her that her white corduroy jacket was sprinkled with the creature's blood. She was shocked. She didn't even realize she had blood on her face and hair until she got home three hours later after the police had questioned her about the incident. Shaking, she explained to her mother why she had been late for supper and why there was a strange odor of pork chops emanating from her hands. Her mother didn't believe her, of course, and punished her severely by cutting her weekly allowance in half, which wasn't much already. Twenty cents can only get you so many pieces of gum.

The next day, the "incident" was called an "accident" on the front page of the paper. She showed her mother the obtuse and airy headline: "ONE HELL OF AN ACCIDENT," as well as the photograph of the grotesque bloody carcass of the pig, spread out perversely on the pavement before the girl in her uniform with her face frozen – her shock visible in the grainy black and white image.

After that, her mother tripled her allowance under one condition: she had to do all her addition and multiplication in the outdoors.

Fandango

Fandango was a turtle who lived in my shoe a long time ago. He was an elderly turtle, very educated and quiet. He was a good tenant until Mr. Pigeonhole moved to the shoe next door. That Pigeonhole was not a pigeon or a hole as his name describes, but an oyster. He said he was a royal descendant of the famous Oysterizer family in Germany, but he spoke no German and wore no gloves, so Fandango was always suspicious.

And curious.

The curiosity burned inside his little shell day and night. Why would an oyster live in a shoe? He wondered. Why would a turtle such as myself live in a shoe? Who is writing this story, for goodness sake? An oyster named Mr. Pigeonhole? What in the sake of all that is good is happening here?

Needless to say, now I have a vacancy in one of my shoes. Fandango has left, very indignant, I might add, and now I am in search for a new tenant.

SHOE FOR RENT

Spacious leather shoe for rent in quiet, safe neighborhood. Rent starts at 4 cents a month and increases with age. Only serious mammals may apply, no silly reptiles please. Contact me by mail only: 555 Textile Road, My Head, WS 42556.

Ursula

Ursula felt it coming long before the tornado failed to stop her soup from boiling over. From the basement, she heard the guillotine at work and then the sighs, the awes, and the pukes that came soon after. Loralee was probably the one who puked, she thought. She was the weakest, and probably the next to get it or at least get nominated.

She didn't like to attend such events so early in the morning. The exaltation would cause her to suffer tragic constipation, preventing her from operating the heavy machinery she needed to operate throughout the day in her farm. She preferred evening gatherings so she could be fully settled and have her tea, crackers, and jam peacefully, with no digestive problems at all.

Long ago, due to a scheduling error, her husband and second child were completed at dawn. To this day she regrets not being able to see their heads roll down the hill and splash into the lake in perfect unison as she had hoped. In her basement she sat, imagining the rising sun in the distance and their shimmering golden hair framing the frozen, puzzled looks on their face. Were their eyes open or closed? She will never know. From then on, she made sure to schedule her family members in the evenings, so she would never miss the spectacle again.

Ursula knew her turn would come, but she had already lived a full life and she didn't mind. She was tired from working in the farm, teaching chickens to spell and goats to add only to slaughter them after they got their diploma. The whole process seemed fruitless, but she knew the townsfolk hadn't nominated her yet because her work was important to the community. Nobody else had the patience to do what she did. Lord knows she tried to pass her knowledge down to her children to keep them safe, but they were too busy helping the poor and going to the university.

What a waste, she thought. What a waste.

In the Event of Occasional Mishaps

The waiting room was filled with empty chairs and disheveled magazines. Maury looked at her watch and re-read the same passage of a Cosmo article about the unilateral support of lacy bras for the thirteenth time in five minutes. Like always, she was the last patient of the day.

The receptionist popped her head up from behind a large window and checked to make sure she was still there.

"She'll be with you in a minute. Thank you for being such a patient...patient," she said with a fake smile. She didn't even bother to wait for Maury's response. Instead, she went back to chatting with her boyfriend online. He had been caught cheating on the bar exam and now had to figure out where to go from there. She sighed and smiled at her perfect manicure with little unicorns and stars floating in the light blue sky of her glossy nail polish.

"That sucks, babe," she typed as the unicorns danced across the keys. How fragile and delicate they galloped. Did unicorns exist? Were they fictional or just extinct, she wondered. She couldn't remember at that very moment. It seemed to her that they must have been real at some point in history. Maybe during the Renaissance?

All Maury could see were little floating strands of the receptionist's fake blonde hair behind a monitor. Back to the same paragraph, the article boasted that the new and improved batch of lacy bras came in all sorts of colors: vermillion, sapphire, midnight black, fuchsia, and cream. They came in all sorts of colors: vermillion, sapphire, midnight black...

Ugh. She didn't even wear a bra. She closed the magazine and threw it on a table.

"Come right in, Ms. Harrison," cried the receptionist. "Dr. Puntrey will see you in exam room seven."

Maury jumped right up and made her way through the labyrinth of empty exam rooms until she reached her own. She sat on a little chair in the corner and wondered how long she was going to wait there. She should've brought the magazine. At least she could look at the pictures or read her horoscope. Now she would never know if she was to ever know true love.

The thought amused her as she sat there in silence. The buzzing of the fluorescent lights above her created a sort of audio cocoon, soothing her in a strange way. She let herself sway from side to side, imagining her hair weaving itself into the invisible fibers of the chrysalis. A certain warmth penetrated her skin and she smirked a little at the thought of her body being enveloped in a white substance made of sound.

Maury knew the doctor had been observing her but she wanted to hang on to that moment a little longer. After all, the doctor had made her wait for over an hour and the least she could do is wait five seconds for her to finish her imaginary sound enclosure.

At last she opened her eyes and the diminutive doctor welcomed her with a simple and honest smile as she propelled herself towards her on a very noisy little stool.

"Ms. Harrison. I'm Dr. Puntrey. I didn't want to interrupt," she said as she reached out her hand.

Maury smiled a little and shook her hand.

"Oh, I was just in my own little world. Very nice to meet you."

"So, it says here you are concerned about a mole in your abdomen. Is that correct?"

"Yes."

"Before you show me the mole, I would like to ask you some questions," the doctor said. "I don't want to get the wrong impression."

"Sure."

"Tell me about the first time you noticed the mole and how it made you feel."

Maury struggled to remember the exact date. It seemed like it had always been with her. Every important moment in her life was punctuated by that little light brown spot on the top left side of her navel. Was it the time she was thrown off her bike when she was thirteen? It was only a tiny little indiscernible speck then. She remembered noticing it when the doctor at the emergency room was wiping away blood from her belly. But was it for the first time?

There was so much blood, but somehow, the discovery of that tiny mark made the pain dissipate and the injury seem trivial as she was hauled away to the operating room. Her mother's tortured face over her and her father holding her hand were the last things she saw and felt before the anesthesia kicked in.

It had been a terrible accident that began as a simple flirtation and ended in a massive collision on a Sunday afternoon. Maury had been riding her bike up and down her street by herself, just letting the thoughts of childhood sway in and out of her head like ocean waves. That very morning, she had put away her favorite bear in the attic. She was a young lady now and she didn't need fluffy toy things in her room. The thought of Woopsie in a dark box collecting dust began to creep in and slowly strangle her heart with guilt and sadness. How stupid. It's just a dumb bear anyway. It didn't even have arms anymore and her mom was tired of sewing his eyes back on every other day.

These thoughts slowly melted away once she spotted the neighbor Erik pretending not to be looking at her from his window. Each time she rode by, the guilt turned to excitement and giddiness yet she tried to remain stoic as was her usual demeanor.

Maury thought he was so dreamy. Every time she would see him at school, with his dark blue eyes and dirty blonde hair, messy and wonderful, her body would explode with excitement and her face would redden and sweat. It was love.

Obviously, she knew it would be ridiculous to just keep riding up and down the street. He would certainly realize she was watching him so she made a deal with herself to just ride by one more time before going back home and snatching Woopsie away from the moths and the spiders in the attic.

As she rode back, Erik was no longer by his window and the curtain was drawn.

Oh well, she thought, resigning herself to the disappointment. Then there he was, riding his bike out of his garage, full speed ahead and straight towards her. It was as though he didn't see her at all. He just plowed right into her.

Although it happened so quickly, she remembers every detail of the accident: her hair covering her face as she flew out of her bike; his hair remaining perfectly still; her fingernail snapping off on impact; and the pain of landing on his handlebars, piercing her abdomen and puncturing her spleen. Then it was darkness until she came to in the hospital. The doctor wiped away the blood and there it was. The mole. The mole in the shape of a sad turtle, she thought. Maybe the drugs had already begun kicking in because she swore she saw the sad turtle turn and give her a little wink.

That accident was the worst thing that had ever happened to her, yet, as she recuperated in her hospital bed, she couldn't help but wonder if Erik had gone out to ride his bike to hang out with her. That meant he had actually noticed her. The pain on her side and the permanent scar on her chin suddenly didn't matter.

The thought of the accident not being considered an accident never crossed her mind. However, her parents doubted the boy's true intentions from the beginning. When they discovered that Erik had a long history of violence, they sued the family. He was sent away to a mental institution and then a group home where he beat his bunk mate to death with a tire iron for breathing too hard and suffocated his pet lizard because it had a mean face.

The Harrisons soon moved to a better neighborhood and Maury never saw him again.

"I think I was thirteen when I first noticed the mole," Maury told the doctor finally, "but it didn't really begin to bother me until last month."

After making a note of it, the doctor stood up and asked her to please take off her shirt and sit on the exam table. Maury did as she was told.

The doctor walked up to her slowly. She adjusted her glasses and with one outstretched pinky, poked around her abdomen, around the mole, then finally put her finger on the mark and held it there. She closed her eyes and slowly began to push until she had created an indentation as deep as Maury's belly button.

Almost like she had fallen asleep, the doctor remained motionless in that position for quite some time. Her breathing had become slow but irregular. Maury looked around the room trying to focus on something, anything that would help her feel less uncomfortable. She looked out the window at the parking lot and saw an ice cream truck had parked right next to her car. She wondered if the driver was a patient in the building and if he was getting good or bad news. He had the perfect "cheer-me-up" or "let's-celebrate" snack right at his fingertips. In case of good news, she would celebrate with an Astro Pop, she thought. In case of bad news, she would find comfort in a Drumstick.

The large ice cream swirly with the happy face on top of the truck rotated and rotated; the happy face appearing and disappearing. Hypnotic.

The doctor sighed a long winded sigh and opened her eyes.

"I'm sorry, Ms. Harrison. I took some Benadryl earlier today because my allergies were acting up after a hike with my German shepherds. I think I happened to doze off at the end there. I apologize. Please put your shirt back on."

The doctor scribbled on her notepad as Maury buttoned her shirt.

"I would like you to go to this lab down the street for some testing before we come up with any conclusions or a diagnosis.

I've also asked the lab to take a stool sample to really get all the information we need," the doctor said.

Stool sample, my ass, she thought. Lunatic.

"Is there anything you could tell me right now?" Maury said and took the lab order form.

"I'd rather not say anything until we have all the results. Make an appointment with the receptionist for a week after you take the tests. See you soon!" Dr. Putney said as she left the room.

Two hours of her life wasted on a narcoleptic doctor obsessed with poop.

As she walked to her car, the swirly was still in motion, mocking her with the disappearing smiling face. Its eyes were stuck in a permanent maniacal state of ecstasy. Its little swoosh of a mouth seemed to say "I'm happy. You are not" over and over again.

Maury got in her car and sighed. Now she had to look for another doctor to look at the mole who she had named Benny after her uncle who always seemed to hang around the house. He had a wacky eye so you never knew where exactly he was looking when he talked to you. Sometimes she would find him in the little shed out back staring at a hammer and axe hanging on the wall.

"Uncle Benny. Mom told me to tell you dinner is ready."

Slowly turning, he would look at her left eye and maybe the tree on her right side and tell her he wasn't staying for dinner. He had bigger fish to fry.

Back at the parking lot, she turned the key and as she was backing out of the parking space, she noticed the driver of the ice cream truck slumped over the steering wheel, sobbing uncontrollably.

She didn't stop the car. She didn't know the man. She shouldn't care why he was crying, but something about that swirly and her recent experience at the doctor's office made her come back around and park again.

The man was not sobbing anymore. He had both hands on the steering wheel and was staring straight ahead, his eyes bloodshot, his nose pink. She noticed he had hairy knuckles and had quite handsome features for an ice cream man.

Building up the necessary courage, Maury got out of her car and knocked on his window.

"No ice cream at this time, ma'am," he said through the closed window.

"I don't want ice cream. I just want to know if you're all right, sir." She said "sir" to retaliate against the "ma'am."

After some time, the man finally turned and stared at her without saying a word. "Mary had a Little Lamb" started blasting out on the megaphone. Still staring into her eyes with a look of both disappointment and shock, he turned on the truck, pulled the shift stick to reverse and started backing up. Maury jumped out of the way before the side mirror hit her on the side of the head. Off he went, loud music, spinning swirly, and all.

What a day. What a day.

———————

Ulysses was the name of the ice cream man. "Ice Cream Man" just happened to be his nickname in the Navy and that's what he became once out of the service. He sometimes wonders if Joe "Dr. Pedo" Jenkins and Pete "the Rocketman" Humphries stayed true to their monikers. Maybe it was destiny.

Destiny is what he blames for all his misery now. There's nothing more unforgiving than fate. That's something he thought about every morning when he woke up with an almost empty bottle of cheap whiskey by his side and a cigarette waiting to be lit on his lips. He always managed to leave just enough liquor in the bottle the night before to immediately cut the debilitating headache in two and satisfy his unquenchable thirst the next day. He always would lay there for a couple of minutes, replaying whatever he could remember about the events of the day in his head, not feeling remorse when he remembered beating up that tough guy behind the 7-11 or feeling elation that he won because the man was twice as big as him. He was too humble to feel pride. He had been drunk too long to feel anything.

That didn't happen this morning.

Ulysses had refrained from drinking the day before so he could wake up fresh and crisp the following morning. He was going to see Trina at her job and ask her to move in so he wanted to have that extra spring in his step which tequila seemed to take away. The pains in his stomach came and went and he almost took a sip of gin out of habit at noon, but the withdrawals weren't as bad as he had imagined. If he could do it for one day perhaps he could do it for two. All he needed was a goal and Trina. Trina. Trina. He could say her name over and over and it would always make him smile the same way.

When he arrived at the medical office building where Trina worked, he realized that all his emotions had increased in intensity. He was actually excited, nervous even, something he hadn't felt in a long time. The tingling sensation of exhilaration reached the tips of his fingers and he felt happy as the elevator took him up to the 6th floor. He could already smell her perfume in the air.

Flowers. Shit. I forgot flowers, he thought. It's okay, he calmed himself. She's allergic.

The brown door at the end of the corridor was all that was between him and Trina now. He opened the door. There she was behind her desk smiling brightly, her dark brown hair in a ponytail like he loved with the UPS guy's hand down her shirt.

"CUT! What asshole didn't lock that door?" a voice said loudly.

The UPS guy took his hand out of her shirt and walked away. "Can someone get me some water?" he yelled at no one in particular.

Still smiling she said, "Hi, Honey! What are you doing here?" She walked up to him and kissed him on the lips.

He looked around and saw people bustling all around, camera equipment, lights. He turned again to look at Trina who looked a little different without the usual haze of alcohol clouding his vision. She was a little older than he remembered, a little less pretty, and her boobs were huge. He didn't remember that at all.

"I didn't realize…What are all these…Are you…?"

Trina laughed and pulled him towards the back of the room. "Oh, I haven't introduced you to my new director. The old director Roger, remember him? The guy with the bad hair flip? Well, he left the company to become legit. Whatever. Anyway, this is Charlie."

Charlie nodded then returned to the novel he was reading about how Nietzsche and Kafka might be the same person on a hyper-biological level.

A man with a long stringy ponytail and a receding hairline walked up to Ulysses with his hand outstretched.

"Oh man. I can't believe it's you! I've been dying to meet you ever since "Pull My Pants Down" and "Scary Pussy." Where have you been, man?"

In this sober, ultra-aware state, clarity seemed to create a fantastical world in which he found himself staring at his other self in an alternate reality.

Drunk Ulysses did some things of which he was not completely aware until this very moment. He had convinced himself that those interesting, sometimes morally deprived things he had done, were only dreams conjured up out of alcohol and drugs. Here, staring him in the face was the realization that he indeed had been a porno king. It had not been just a drunken fantasy.

"I guess I haven't been drinking the right stuff, man," he said.

Suddenly, the assistant director yelled "places everyone!"

"Sorry, babe. I've got to go," said Trina as she kissed him and walked away.

"Will I see you later at Lenny's?" she asked, but she didn't wait for his reply. She was already kissing the UPS guy with her hand down his shorts by the time Ulysses muttered a sober "of course."